Bob the Builder™

Travis and Scoop's Big Race

A Lift-the-Flap Story

by
Sarah Willson

illustrated by
Giuseppe Castellano

SIMON SPOTLIGHT
An imprint of Simon & Schuster Children's Publishing Division
New York   London   Toronto   Sydney   Singapore
1230 Avenue of the Americas, New York, New York 10020
© 2003 HIT Entertainment PLC and Keith Chapman. All rights reserved.
Bob the Builder and all related titles, logos, and characters are trademarks of HIT Entertainment PLC and Keith Chapman.
Photos by Hot Animation. All rights reserved, including the right of reproduction in whole or in part in any form.
SIMON SPOTLIGHT and colophon are registered trademarks of Simon & Schuster.
Manufactured in China   ISBN 0-689-85302-5   First Edition

2 4 6 8 10 9 7 5 3 1

Scoop and Roley had just finished fixing a road near Farmer Pickles's farm.

"Phew! We sure make a fast team!" Scoop said to Roley.

Spud and Travis were listening nearby. "You think you're fast?" called Spud. "Travis and I are faster workers than you two!"

"That's right," Travis added, "Farmer Pickles says I'm the fastest tractor he's ever had!"

"Let's have a race and find out who's *really* faster!" said Scoop.

Scoop and Roley hurried back to the building yard to tell Bob about the big race.

"Now Travis and Scoop will know which way to go."

"A race!" cried Bob. "How exciting!"
Bob and Muck got right to work
setting up a path for the race.

Travis looked worried. "Uh, Spud, Farmer Pickles didn't exactly say I was the fastest tractor," Travis whispered. "He said I was the fastest *talker.*"

"Oh, Travis!" said Spud with a groan. "How will you ever beat Scoop?"

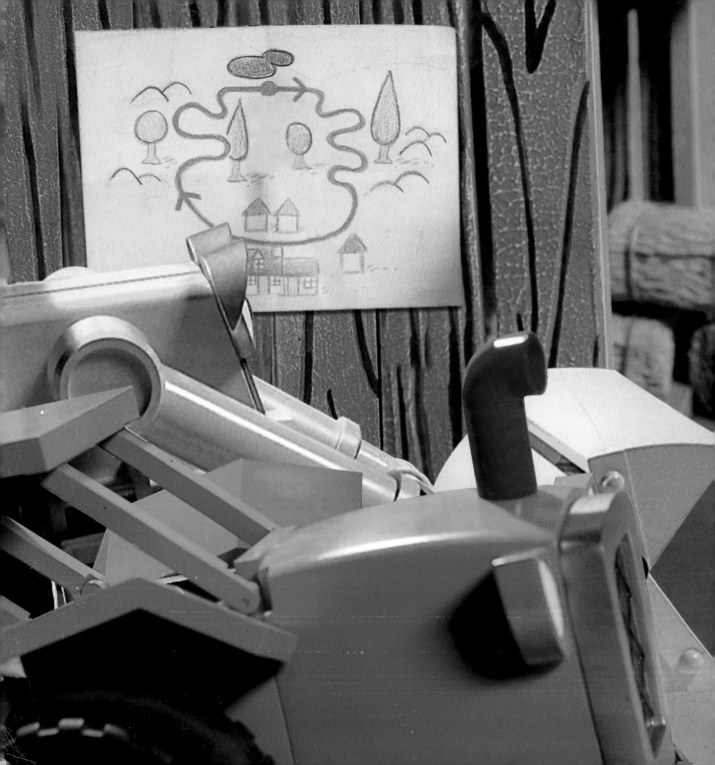

It was finally time for the race. "Ready . . . set . . . GO!" called Bob.
Scoop and Travis took off. Nobody saw Spud creep away.

"If Travis is going to win the race, he'll need a little help from me," said Spud as he set up a brick wall.

Scoop was in the lead. Suddenly he screeched to a halt. What was that blocking the way? It looked like a brick wall! He gave it a nudge with his digger, and it fell over. Travis whooshed past him.

When Spud saw that Scoop was in the lead again, he decided to take some action. He quickly fiddled with the traffic light controls . . . .

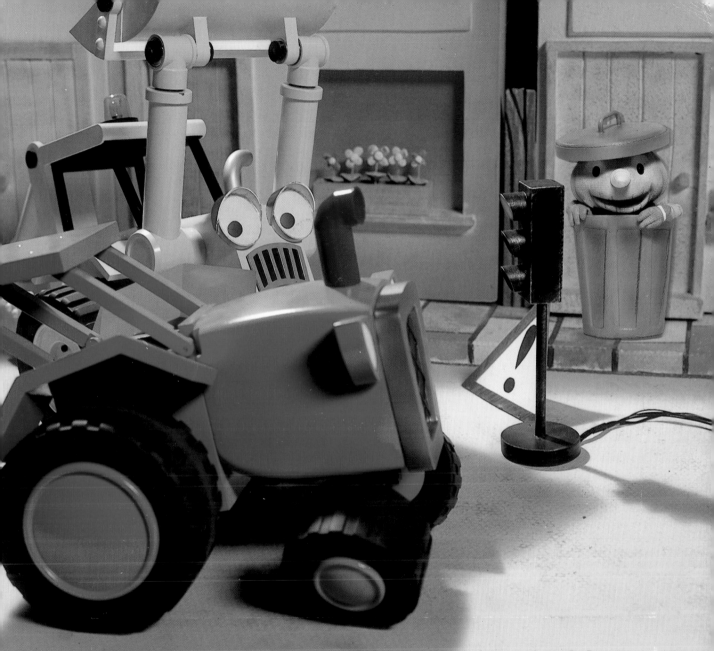

Scoop was winning! But then he saw something ahead. It was a traffic light. And it had just turned red!

While Scoop waited for the light to turn green, Travis passed him.

Speedy Scoop soon caught up with Travis. But what was in the road now? Scoop hit his brakes in the nick of time. There was a roadblock! Travis raced right around it toward the finish line.

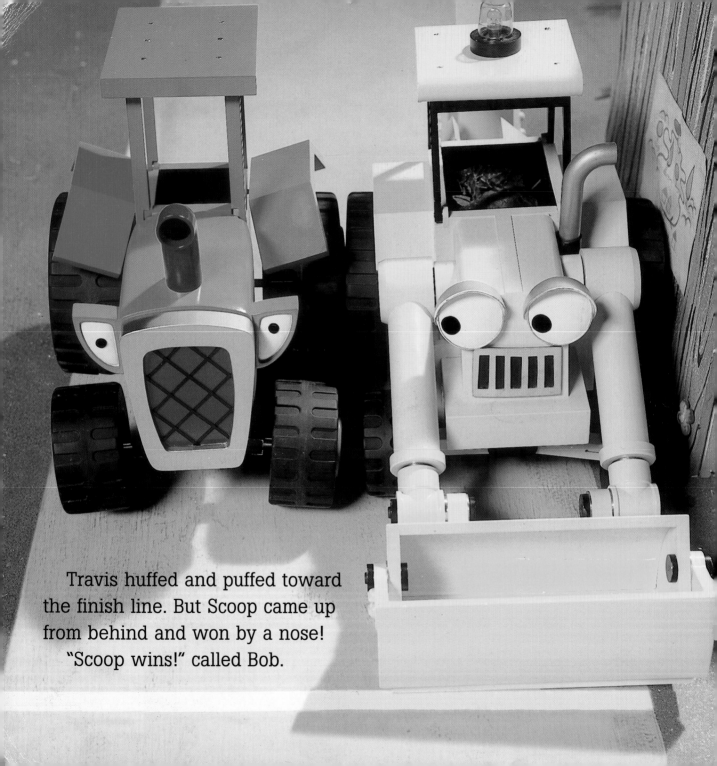

Travis huffed and puffed toward the finish line. But Scoop came up from behind and won by a nose! "Scoop wins!" called Bob.